THE CAT, THE DOG, LITTLE RED, THE EXPLODING EGGS, THE WOLF AND GRANDMA'S WARDROBE

Diane and Christyan Fox

words & pictures

There was once a sweet little maid who lived with her father and mother in a pretty little cottage at the edge of the village.

She always wore a red cloak with a hood, which suited her so well that everybody called her Little Red Riding Hood.

What's this?

It's a story about a little girl who always wears a red cloak with a hood.

COOL! I love stories
about superheroes.
What's her
special power?

She doesn't have
any special powers.
It's not that kind
of a story.

And can you stop
doing that, please?

So, what
happens?

Well, one morning
her mother asked
Red Riding Hood to
take a basket of
eggs, butter, cake,
and dainties to
her grandmother.

So, Kindness is her special power? Does she hypnotize bad guys into being nice?

And what's a "dainty"?

A dainty is like a... well... it's a kind of small... er...

Look, do you want to hear this story or not?

. So, where was I?

Little Red Riding Hood was on her way to Grandma's house when she met a wolf...

A WOLF! EXCELLENT!

They're always the bad guys in stories like this.

I bet she zaps him with her KINDNESS RAY.

ZZZZ!!

She does **NOT** have a
KINDNESS RAY...
she has a basket of
eggs and butter and
cakes and dainties.

How does she fight
crime, then? Is it
like a cool kind of
flying gadget basket?

Are they exploding
eggs? Can she whack
him with a dainty?

THERE'S **NO** KINDNESS RAY, **NO** FLYING BASKET AND **NO** EXPLODING EGGS.

SHE'S JUST A SWEET LITTLE GIRL WITH TERRIBLE FASHION SENSE ON HER WAY TO SEE HER GRANDMOTHER.

OK, ok... so let's hear the rest of the story.

Well, the Wolf asked Red Riding Hood where she was going and she said, "Grandma's house," so the Wolf said goodbye and secretly headed off to Grandma's house...

Hang on...
why doesn't the Wolfman try to eat Hood Girl there and then?

You're doing this on purpose, aren't you? How should I know why he didn't try to eat her?

Hmm... I wonder if it's because old ladies taste better than little girls?

Anyway, the Wolf arrived at Grandma's cottage and saw the old lady lying in bed. She jumped up when she saw the Wolf and locked herself in the wardrobe.

I think the Wolf needs to think bigger if he's going to be a super-villain.

Maybe he could rob a bank on the way to Grandma's house?

Are you
listening
at all?

Yep.

OK, so Grandma leapt up out of bed and locked herself in the wardrobe to be safe.

Then the Wolf put on some of Grandma's clothes and climbed into the bed, waiting for Little Red Riding Hood to arrive.

Hang on...

so now you're saying he DOES want to eat her?

Yes... anyway, this is my favourite bit. She arrived and said, "What big eyes you have Grandma," and the Wolf replied, "All the better to see you with."

She's not very bright, is she? I mean, if there were a Wolf dressed up as MY grandma, I might have noticed right away.

...and Little Red Riding Hood
said, "What a big nose
you have, Grandma."

And the Wolf replied,
"All the better to smell
you with, my dear."

Let me see
that book...

...And she said, "What big teeth you have, Grandma," and the Wolf said...

ALL THE BETTER TO EAT YOU UP!

YIKES!

But just at the last moment,
Little Red Riding Hood's
father arrived and

CHOPPED OFF THE WOLF'S HEAD WITH AN AXE!

GULP!

And they all lived happily ever after.

I'm not sure that the Wolf was very happy in the end.

So, let's see if I have this right...

The Red Hood is on her way to help an old lady when she meets the Wolfman, whose evil plan it is to eat all the old ladies in the world because he likes dressing up in girls' clothes. He and Red have a big battle over the dainties and Red's father chops Wolfie with an axe.

Well... sort of...

It's not a very
nice story, is it?

Are you absolutely
sure this is a
children's book?

RIGHT, THAT'S IT...
I'm leaving.
Find your own
books to read.

Just one
last
question...

What?

Is Grandma
still in the
wardrobe?